To ....

For being good.

Merry Christmas!

From Santa

Santa is coming to Texas

Written by Steve Smallman
Illustrated by Robert Dunn

Copyright © Hometown World Ltd. 2019

Published by Sourcebooks Jabberwocky,
an imprint of Sourcebooks, Inc.
P.O. Box 4410, Naperville, Illinois 60567-4410
(630) 961-3900
jabberwockykids.com

Date of Production: May 2019
Run Number: 5014816
Printed and bound in China (1010)
10 9 8 7 6 5 4 3 2 1

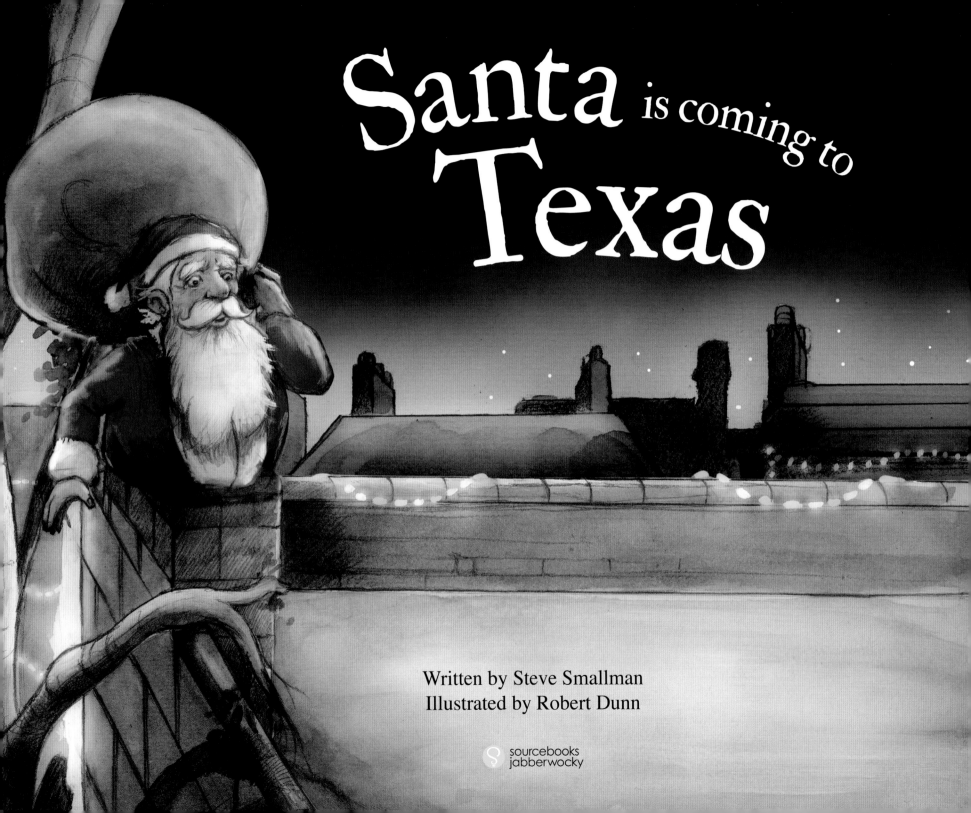

Santa is coming to Texas

Written by Steve Smallman
Illustrated by Robert Dunn

sourcebooks
jabberwocky

"Well?"

boomed Santa. "Have all the children from Texas been good this year?"

"Well…uh…mostly," answered the little old elf, as he bustled across the busy workshop to Santa's desk.

Santa peered down at the elf from behind the tall, teetering piles of letters that the children of Texas had sent him.

"Mostly?" asked Santa, looking over the top of his glasses.

"Yes…but they've all been especially good in the last few days!" said the elf.

"Jolly good!" chuckled Santa.
"Then we'd better get their presents loaded up!"

Even though the sack of presents was

really, really big

and the elves were **really, really** small,

they seemed to have no trouble loading it onto Santa's sleigh.
Though how they managed to fit such a big sack onto one little sleigh
even they didn't know. But somehow they did.

"Splendid!" boomed Santa. "We're ready to go!"

"Er...not quite, Santa," said the little old elf. "One of our reindeer is missing!"

"Missing?

Which reindeer is missing?" asked Santa.

"The youngest one, Santa," said the elf. "It's his first flight tonight. I've called him and called him, but..."

Just then, a young reindeer strolled up, munching on a large carrot.

"Where have you been?"

asked Santa.

But the youngest reindeer was crunching so loudly that it was no wonder he hadn't heard the little old elf calling.

"Oh well, never mind," said Santa, giving the reindeer a little wink. He took out his Santa-nav and tapped in the coordinates for Texas.

"This will guide us to Texas in no time."

CRUNCH!
CRUNCH!
CRUNCH!

With a flick of the reins and a jerk of the harness, off they went, racing through the sky.

"Ho, ho, ho!"

laughed Santa.

"We'll soon have these presents delivered to the Lone Star State!"

Santa's sleigh flew through the starry night, heading south across the Arctic Ocean. On they flew in the crisp, wintry air, crossing over Canada. In the wink of an eye, the sleigh was flying above Oklahoma, and then over Fort Worth. The youngest reindeer was very excited. He had never been away from the North Pole before.

They were just nearing Round Rock
when, suddenly, they ran into a thick fog.
Mist swirled around the sleigh.

They couldn't see a thing!

The youngest reindeer was getting a bit worried,
but Santa didn't seem concerned.

"In two miles..."

said the Santa-nav in a bossy lady's voice,

"...keep left at the next star."

"But, ma'am," Santa blustered, "I can't see any stars in all this fog!"
Soon they were

hopelessly lost!

Ding-dong!
Ding-dong!

Then, through the foggy blanket, the youngest reindeer heard a faint, ringing sound.

Ding-dong!

He looked over at the old reindeer with the red nose. But he had his head down.

(Red nose...I wonder who that could be?)

Ding-dong!
Ding-dong!

Ding-dong! Ding-dong!

There was that sound again, like church bells ringing. The youngest reindeer turned around to look at Santa. But Santa wasn't listening. He seemed to be arguing with a little box with buttons on it.

With a flick of the harness and a jerk of the reins, the youngest reindeer gave a sharp **TUG** and headed off toward the sound of the bells, pulling Santa and his sleigh behind him!

"Whoa!"

cried Santa, pulling his hat straight. "What's going on?" Then, to his surprise, he heard the ringing sound.

"Well done, young reindeer!" he shouted cheerfully. "It must be the University of Texas Tower. Don't worry, children, Santa is coming!"

Then, suddenly...

CRUNCH!

The sleigh hit something as it plummeted through the fog.

"You have arrived!" said the Santa-nav unhelpfully.

The reindeer **PULLED** with all their might until, at last,
with a screeching noise, the sleigh scraped clear of the
dome and Santa steered them safely past the Paramount,
over the Congress Bridge, around the Umlauf,
and down into Zilker Park.

Luckily, there was
no real damage done,
but the packages had all been
jumbled up. Santa quickly sorted
out the presents into order again.

"All right," said Santa. "Thanks
to this young reindeer I know where
we are now. Don't worry, children,

Santa is coming!"

Santa drove his sleigh expertly from rooftop to rooftop all over Texas, popping in and out of chimneys as fast as he could go.

(Which was pretty fast for a chubby fellow!)

There were big chimneys in Amarillo, and small chimneys in Houston. He squeezed down thin chimneys in San Antonio and plummeted down fat chimneys in Fairview.

The youngest reindeer was amazed at how quickly they went. Santa never seemed to get tired at all! And it looked like the children in Texas were going to be very lucky this year! But the youngest reindeer was starting to feel a bit weary and quite hungry, too!

He piled them under the Christmas trees
and carefully filled up the stockings
with surprises.

In house after house, Santa delved
inside his sack for packages of
every shape and size.

Santa took a little bite out of each cookie,
a tiny sip of milk, wiped his beard,
and popped the carrots into his sack.

In house after house, the good children
of Texas had left out a large plate
of cookies, a small glass of milk,
and a big, crunchy carrot.

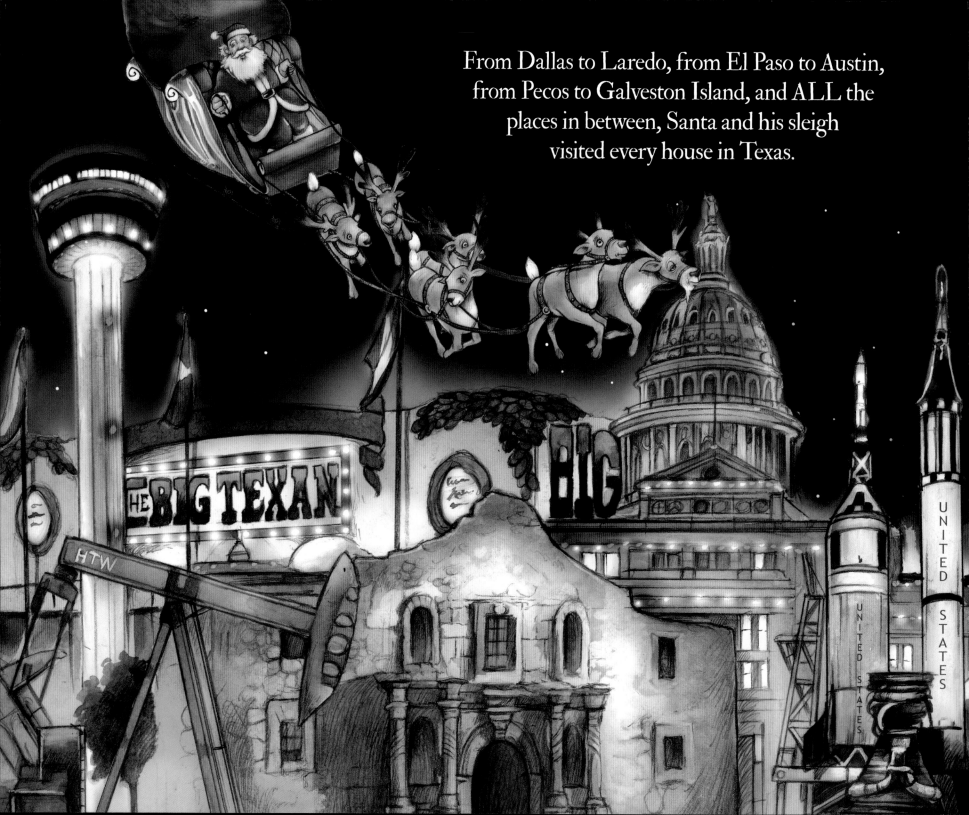

From Dallas to Laredo, from El Paso to Austin,
from Pecos to Galveston Island, and ALL the
places in between, Santa and his sleigh
visited every house in Texas.

Santa delivered presents to Andrew, Alison, Anna, Arabella, Archie, Ashley...the list went on and on!...Zac, Zara, Zeb, Zoe, Zybil.

(Zybil? That must be a spelling mistake, surely!)

Finally, Santa had delivered the
last present on his long Texas list.

"Great moons and stars!" sighed
Santa. "It's past midnight and my sack seems as
heavy as ever! I hope I haven't forgotten anyone."

Santa opened his sack to check...but it was full
of juicy, crunchy carrots!

Santa divided the carrots among all the reindeer.
"Well done!" he said, patting the youngest reindeer gently on the nose.

But the youngest reindeer didn't hear him...he was too busy munching!

Then it was time to set off for home. Santa reset his Santa-nav
once more to the North Pole, and soon they were speeding
over Dallas through the crisp, starry night.